Genesis

H. Beam Piper

Contents

GENESIS

BY
H. Beam Piper

GENESIS
By H. Beam Piper
FEATURE NOVELET
OF LOST WORLDS

Was this ill-fated expedition the end of a proud, old race--or the beginning of a new one?

There are strange gaps in our records of the past. We find traces of man-like things--but, suddenly, man appears, far too much developed to be the "next step" in a well-linked chain of evolutionary evidence. Perhaps something like the events of this story furnishes the answer to the riddle.

Aboard the ship, there was neither day nor night; the hours slipped gently by, as vistas of star-gemmed blackness slid across the visiscreens. For the crew, time had some meaning--one watch on duty and two off. But for the thousand-odd colonists, the men and women who were to be the spearhead of migration to a new and friendlier planet, it had none. They slept, and played, worked at such tasks as they could invent, and slept again, while the huge ship followed her plotted trajectory.

Kalvar Dard, the army officer who would lead them in their new home, had as little to do as any of his followers. The ship's officers had all the responsibility for the voyage, and, for the first time in over five years, he had none at all. He was finding the unaccustomed idleness more wearying than the hectic work of loading the ship before the blastoff from Doorsha. He went over his landing and security plans again, and found no probable emergency unprepared for. Dard wandered about the ship, talking to groups of his colonists, and found morale even better than he had hoped. He spent hours staring into the forward visiscreens, watching the disc of Tareesh, the planet of his destination, grow larger and plainer ahead.

Now, with the voyage almost over, he was in the cargo-hold just aft of the Number Seven bulkhead, with six girls to help him, checking construction material which would be needed immediately after landing. The stuff had all been checked two or three times before, but there was no harm in going over it again. It furnished an occupation to fill in the time; it gave Kalvar Dard an excuse for surrounding himself with half a dozen charming girls, and the girls seemed to enjoy being with him. There was tall blonde Olva, the electromagnetician; pert little Varnis, the machinist's helper; Kyna, the surgeon's-aide; dark-haired Analea; Dorita, the accountant; plump little Eldra, the armament technician. At the moment, they were all sitting on or around the desk in the corner of the store-room, going over the inventory when they were not just gabbling.

"Well, how about the rock-drill bitts?" Dorita was asking earnestly, trying to stick to business. "Won't we need them almost as soon as we're off?"

"Yes, we'll have to dig temporary magazines for our explosives, small-arms and artillery ammunition, and storage-pits for our fissionables and radioactives," Kalvar Dard replied. "We'll have to have safe places for that stuff ready before it can be unloaded; and if we run into hard rock near the surface, we'll have to drill holes for blasting-shots."

"The drilling machinery goes into one of those prefabricated sheds," Eldra considered. "Will there be room in it for all the bitts, too?"

Kalvar Dard shrugged. "Maybe. If not, we'll cut poles and build racks for them outside. The bitts are nono-steel; they can be stored in the open."

"If there are poles to cut," Olva added.

"I'm not worrying about that," Kalvar Dard replied. "We have a pretty fair idea of conditions on Tareesh; our astronomers have been making telescopic observations for the past fifteen centuries. There's a pretty big Arctic ice-cap, but it's been receding slowly, with a wide belt of what's believed to be open grassland to the south of it, and a belt of what's assumed to be evergreen forest south of that. We plan to land somewhere in the northern hemisphere, about the grassland-forest line. And since Tareesh is richer in water that Doorsha, you mustn't think of grassland in terms of our wire-grass plains, or forests in terms of our brush thickets. The vegetation should be much more luxuriant."

"If there's such a large polar ice-cap, the summers ought to be fairly cool, and the winters cold," Varnis reasoned. "I'd think that would mean fur-bearing animals. Colonel, you'll have to shoot me something with a nice soft fur; I like furs."

Kalvar Dard chuckled. "Shoot you nothing, you can shoot your own furs. I've seen your carbine and pistol scores," he began.

$$* \qquad * \qquad * \qquad * \qquad *$$

There was a sudden suck of air, disturbing the papers on the desk. They all turned to see one of the ship's rocket-boat bays open; a young Air Force lieutenant named Seldar Glav, who would be staying on Tareesh with them to pilot their aircraft, emerged from an open airlock.

"Don't tell me you've been to Tareesh and back in that thing," Olva greeted him.

Seldar Glav grinned at her. "I could have been, at that; we're only twenty or thirty planetary calibers away, now. We ought to be entering Tareeshan atmosphere by the middle of the next watch. I was only checking the boats, to make sure they'll be ready to launch.... Colonel Kalvar, would you mind stepping over here? There's something I think you should look at, sir."

Kalvar Dard took one arm from around Analea's waist and lifted the other from Varnis' shoulder, sliding off the desk. He followed Glav into the boat-bay; as they went through the airlock, the cheerfulness left the young lieutenant's face.

"I didn't want to say anything in front of the girls, sir," he began, "but I've been checking boats to make sure we can make a quick getaway. Our meteor-security's gone out. The detectors are deader then the Fourth Dynasty, and the blasters won't synchronize.... Did you hear a big thump, about a half an hour ago, Colonel?"

"Yes, I thought the ship's labor-crew was shifting heavy equipment in the hold aft of us. What was it, a meteor-hit?"

"It was. Just aft of Number Ten bulkhead. A meteor about the size of the nose of that rocket-boat."

Kalvar Dard whistled softly. "Great Gods of Power! The detectors must be dead, to pass up anything like that.... Why wasn't a boat-stations call sent out?"

"Captain Vlazil was unwilling to risk starting a panic, sir," the Air Force officer replied. "Really, I'm exceeding my orders in mentioning it to you, but I thought you should know...."

Kalvar Dard swore. "It's a blasted pity Captain Vlazil didn't try thinking! Gold-braided quarter-wit! Maybe his crew might panic, but my people wouldn't.... I'm going to call the control-room and have it out with him. By the Ten Gods...!"

*   *   *   *   *

He ran through the airlock and back into the hold, starting toward the inter-com-phone beside the desk. Before he could reach it, there was another heavy jar, rocking the entire ship. He, and Seldar Glav, who had followed him out of the boat-bay, and the six girls, who had risen on hearing their commander's angry voice, were all tumbled into a heap. Dard surged to his feet, dragging Kyna up along with him; together, they helped the others to rise. The ship was suddenly filled with jangling bells, and the red danger-lights on the ceiling were flashing on and off.

"Attention! Attention!" the voice of some officer in the control-room blared out of the intercom-speaker. "The ship has just been hit by a large meteor! All compartments between bulkheads Twelve and Thirteen are sealed off. All persons between bulkheads Twelve and Thirteen, put on oxygen helmets and plug in at the nearest phone connection. Your air is leaking, and you can't get out, but if you put on oxygen equipment immediately, you'll be all right. We'll get you out as soon as we can, and in any case, we are only a few hours out of Tareeshan atmosphere. All persons in Compartment Twelve, put on...."

Kalvar Dard was swearing evilly. "That does it! That does it for good!... Anybody else in this compartment, below the living quarter level?"

"No, we're the only ones," Analea told him.

"The people above have their own boats; they can look after themselves. You girls, get in that boat, in there. Glav, you and I'll try to warn the people above...."

There was another jar, heavier than the one which had preceded it, throwing them all down again. As they rose, a new voice was shouting over the public-address system:

"***Abandon ship! Abandon ship!*** The converters are backfiring, and rocket-fuel is leaking back toward the engine-rooms! An explosion is imminent! Abandon ship, all hands!"

Kalvar Dard and Seldar Glav grabbed the girls and literally threw them through the hatch, into the rocket-boat. Dard pushed Glav in ahead of him, then jumped in. Before he had picked himself up, two or three of the girls were at the hatch, dogging the cover down.

"All right, Glav, blast off!" Dard ordered. "We've got to be at least a hundred miles from this ship when she blows, or we'll blow with her!"

"Don't I know!" Seldar Glav retorted over his shoulder, racing for the controls. "Grab hold of something, everybody; I'm going to fire all jets at once!"

An instant later, while Kalvar Dard and the girls clung to stanchions and pieces of fixed furniture, the boat shot forward out of its housing. When Dard's head had cleared, it was in free flight.

"How was that?" Glav yelled. "Everybody all right?" He hesitated for a moment. "I think I blacked out for about ten seconds."

Kalvar Dard looked the girls over. Eldra was using a corner of her smock to stanch a nosebleed, and Olva had a bruise over one eye. Otherwise, everybody was in good shape.

"Wonder we didn't all black out, permanently," he said. "Well, put on the visiscreens, and let's see what's going on outside. Olva, get on the radio and try to see if anybody else got away."

"Set course for Tareesh?" Glav asked. "We haven't fuel enough to make it back to Doorsha."

"I was afraid of that," Dard nodded. "Tareesh it is; northern hemisphere, daylight side. Try to get about the edge of the temperate zone, as near water as you can...."

2

They were flung off their feet again, this time backward along the boat. As they picked themselves up, Seldar Glav was shaking his head, sadly. "That was the ship going up," he said; "the blast must have caught us dead astern."

"All right." Kalvar Dard rubbed a bruised forehead. "Set course for Tareesh, then cut out the jets till we're ready to land. And get the screens on, somebody; I want to see what's happened."

The screens glowed; then full vision came on. The planet on which they would land loomed huge before them, its north pole toward them, and its single satellite on the port side. There was no sign of any rocket-boat in either side screen, and the rear-view screen was a blur of yellow flame from the jets.

"Cut the jets, Glav," Dard repeated. "Didn't you hear me?"

"But I did, sir!" Seldar Glav indicated the firing-panel. Then he glanced at the rear-view screen. "The gods help us! It's yellow flame; the jets are burning out!"

Kalvar Dard had not boasted idly when he had said that his people would not panic. All the girls went white, and one or two gave low cries of consternation, but that was all.

"What happens next?" Analea wanted to know. "Do we blow, too?"

"Yes, as soon as the fuel-line burns up to the tanks."

"Can you land on Tareesh before then?" Dard asked.

"I can try. How about the satellite? It's closer."

"It's also airless. Look at it and see for yourself," Kalvar Dard advised. "Not enough mass to hold an atmosphere."

Glav looked at the army officer with new respect. He had always been inclined to think of the Frontier Guards as a gang of scientifically illiterate dirk-and-pistol bravos. He fiddled for a while with instruments on the panel; an automatic computer figured the distance to the planet, the boat's velocity, and the time needed for a landing.

"We have a chance, sir," he said. "I think I can set down in about thirty minutes; that should give us about ten minutes to get clear of the boat, before she blows up."

"All right; get busy, girls," Kalvar Dard said. "Grab everything we'll need. Arms and ammunition first; all of them you can find. After that, warm clothing, bedding, tools and food."

With that, he jerked open one of the lockers and began pulling out weapons.

He buckled on a pistol and dagger, and handed other weapon-belts to the girls behind him. He found two of the heavy big-game rifles, and several bandoliers of ammunition for them. He tossed out carbines, and boxes of carbine and pistol cartridges. He found two bomb-bags, each containing six light anti-personnel grenades and a big demolition-bomb. Glancing, now and then, at the forward screen, he caught glimpses of blue sky and green-tinted plains below.

"All right!" the pilot yelled. "We're coming in for a landing! A couple of you stand by to get the hatch open."

There was a jolt, and all sense of movement stopped. A cloud of white smoke drifted past the screens. The girls got the hatch open; snatching up weapons and bedding-wrapped bundles they all scrambled up out of the boat.

There was fire outside. The boat had come down upon a grassy plain; now the grass was burning from the heat of the jets. One by one, they ran forward along the top of the rocket-boat, jumping down to the ground clear of the blaze. Then, with every atom of strength they possessed they ran away from the doomed boat.

* * * * *

The ground was rough, and the grass high, impeding them. One of the girls tripped and fell; without pausing, two others pulled her to her feet, while another snatched up and slung the carbine she had dropped. Then, ahead, Kalvar Dard saw a deep gully, through which a little stream trickled.

They huddled together at the bottom of it, waiting, for what seemed like a long while. Then a gentle tremor ran through the ground, and swelled to a sickening, heaving shock. A roar of almost palpable sound swept over them, and a flash of blue-white light dimmed the sun above. The sound, the shock, and the searing light did not pass away at once; they continued for seconds that seemed like an eternity. Earth and stones pelted down around them; choking dust rose. Then the thunder and the earth-shock were over; above, incandescent vapors swirled, and darkened into an overhanging pall of smoke and dust.

For a while, they crouched motionless, too stunned to speak. Then shaken nerves steadied and jarred brains cleared. They all rose weakly. Trickles of earth were still coming down from the sides of the gully, and the little stream, which had been clear and sparkling, was roiled with mud. Mechanically, Kalvar Dard brushed the dust from his clothes and looked to his weapons.

"That was just the fuel-tank of a little Class-3 rocket-boat," he said. "I wonder what the explosion of the ship was like." He thought for a moment before continuing. "Glav, I think I know why our jets burned out. We were stern-on to the ship when she blew; the blast drove our flame right back through the jets."

"Do you think the explosion was observed from Doorsha?" Dorita inquired, more concerned about the practical aspects of the situation. "The ship, I mean. After all, we have no means of communication, of our own."

"Oh, I shouldn't doubt it; there were observatories all around the planet watching our ship," Kalvar Dard said. "They probably know all about it, by now. But if any of you are thinking about the chances of rescue, forget it. We're stuck here."

"That's right. There isn't another human being within fifty million miles," Seldar Glav said. "And that was the first and only space-ship ever built. It took fifty years to build her, and even allowing twenty for research that wouldn't have to be duplicated, you can figure when we can expect another one."

"The answer to that one is, never. The ship blew up in space; fifty years' effort and fifteen hundred people gone, like that." Kalvar Dard snapped his fingers. "So now, they'll try to keep Doorsha habitable for a few more thousand years by irrigation, and forget about immigrating to Tareesh."

"Well, maybe, in a hundred thousand years, our descendants will build a ship and go to Doorsha, then," Olva considered.

"Our descendants?" Eldra looked at her in surprize. "You mean, then...?"

*   *   *   *   *

Kyna chuckled. "Eldra, you are an awful innocent, about anything that doesn't have a breech-action or a recoil-mechanism," she said. "Why do you think the women on this expedition outnumbered the men seven to five, and why do you think there were so many obstetricians and pediatricians in the med. staff? We were sent out to put a human population on Tareesh, weren't we? Well, here we are."

"But.... Aren't we ever going to...?" Varnis began. "Won't we ever see anybody else, or do anything but just live here, like animals, without machines or ground-cars or aircraft or houses or anything?" Then she began to sob bitterly.

Analea, who had been cleaning a carbine that had gotten covered with loose earth during the explosion, laid it down and went to Varnis, putting her arm around the other girl and comforting her. Kalvar Dard picked up the carbine she had laid down.

"Now, let's see," he began. "We have two heavy rifles, six carbines, and eight pistols, and these two bags of bombs. How much ammunition, counting what's in our belts, do we have?"

They took stock of their slender resources, even Varnis joining in the task, as he had hoped she would. There were over two thousand rounds for the pistols, better than fifteen hundred for the carbines, and four hundred for the two big-game guns. They had some spare clothing, mostly space-suit undergarments, enough bed-robes, one hand-axe, two flashlights, a first-aid kit, and three atomic lighters. Each one had a combat-dagger. There was enough tinned food for about a week.

"We'll have to begin looking for game and edible plants, right away," Glav considered. "I suppose there is game, of some sort; but our ammunition won't last forever."

"We'll have to make it last as long as we can; and we'll have to begin improvising weapons," Dard told him. "Throwing-spears, and throwing-axes. If we can find metal, or any recognizable ore that we can smelt, we'll use that; if not, we'll use chipped stone. Also, we can learn to make snares and traps, after we learn the habits of the animals on this planet. By the time the ammunition's gone, we ought to have learned to do without firearms."

"Think we ought to camp here?"

Kalvar Dard shook his head. "No wood here for fuel, and the blast will have scared away all the game. We'd better go upstream; if we go down, we'll find the water roiled with mud and unfit to drink. And if the game on this planet behave like the game-herds on the wastelands of Doorsha, they'll run for high ground when frightened."

Varnis rose from where she had been sitting. Having mastered her emotions, she was making a deliberate effort to show it.

"Let's make up packs out of this stuff," she suggested. "We can use the bedding and spare clothing to bundle up the food and ammunition."

They made up packs and slung them, then climbed out of the gully. Off to the left, the grass was burning in a wide circle around the crater left by the explosion of the rocket-boat. Kalvar Dard, carrying one of the heavy rifles, took the lead. Beside and a little behind him, Analea walked, her carbine ready. Glav, with the other heavy rifle, brought up in the rear, with Olva covering for him, and between, the other girls walked, two and two.

Ahead, on the far horizon, was a distance-blue line of mountains. The little company turned their faces toward them and moved slowly away, across the empty sea of grass.

3

They had been walking, now, for five years. Kalvar Dard still led, the heavy rifle cradled in the crook of his left arm and a sack of bombs slung from his shoulder, his eyes forever shifting to right and left searching for hidden danger. The clothes in which he had jumped from the rocket-boat were patched and ragged; his shoes had been replaced by high laced buskins of smoke-tanned hide. He was bearded, now, and his hair had been roughly trimmed with the edge of his dagger.

Analea still walked beside him, but her carbine was slung, and she carried three spears with chipped flint heads; one heavy weapon, to be thrown by hand or used for stabbing, and two light javelins to be thrown with the aid of the hooked throwing-stick Glav had invented. Beside her trudged a four-year old boy, hers and Dard's, and on her back, in a fur-lined net bag, she carried their six-month-old baby.

In the rear, Glav still kept his place with the other big-game gun, and Olva walked beside him with carbine and spears; in front of them, their three-year-old daughter toddled. Between vanguard and rearguard, the rest of the party walked: Varnis, carrying her baby on her back, and Dorita, carrying a baby and leading two other children. The baby on her back had cost the life of Kyna in childbirth; one of the others had been left motherless when Eldra had been killed by the Hairy People.

*　　*　　*　　*　　*

That had been two years ago, in the winter when they had used one of their two demolition-bombs to blast open a cavern in the mountains. It had been a hard winter; two children had died, then--Kyna's firstborn, and the little son of Kalvar Dard and Dorita. It had been their first encounter with the Hairy People, too.

Eldra had gone outside the cave with one of the skin water-bags, to fill it at the spring. It had been after sunset, but she had carried her pistol, and no one had thought of danger until they heard the two quick shots, and the scream. They had all rushed out, to find four shaggy, manlike things tearing at Eldra with hands and teeth, another lying dead, and a sixth huddled at one side, clutching its abdomen and whimpering. There had been a quick flurry of shots that had felled all four of the assailants, and Seldar Glav had finished the wounded creature with his dagger, but Eldra was dead. They had built a cairn of stones over her body, as they had done over the bodies of the two children killed by the cold. But, after an examination to see what sort of things they were, they had tumbled the bodies of the Hairy People over the cliff. These had been too bestial to bury as befitted human dead, but too manlike to skin and eat as game.

Since then, they had often found traces of the Hairy People, and when they met with them, they killed them without mercy. These were great shambling parodies of humanity, long-armed, short-legged, twice as heavy as men, with close-set reddish eyes and heavy bone-crushing jaws. They may have been incredibly debased humans, or perhaps beasts on the very threshold of manhood. From what he had seen of conditions on this planet, Kalvar Dard suspected the latter to be the case. In a million or so years, they might evolve into something like humanity. Already, the Hairy ones had learned the use of fire, and of chipped crude stone implements--mostly heavy triangular choppers to be used in the hand, without helves.

Twice, after that night, the Hairy People had attacked them--once while they were on the march, and once in camp. Both assaults had been beaten off without loss to themselves, but at cost of precious ammunition. Once they had caught a band of ten of them swimming a river on logs; they had picked them all off from the bank with their carbines. Once, when Kalvar Dard and Analea had been scouting alone, they had come upon a dozen of them huddled around a fire and had wiped them out with a single grenade. Once, a large band of Hairy People hunted them for two days, but only twice had they come close, and both times, a single shot had sent them all scampering. That had been after the bombing of the group around the fire. Dard was convinced that the beings possessed the rudiments of a language, enough to communicate a few simple ideas, such as the fact that this little tribe of aliens were dangerous in the extreme.

*   *   *   *   *

There were Hairy People about now; for the past five days, moving northward through the forest to the open grasslands, the people of Kalvar Dard had found traces of them. Now, as they came out among the seedling growth at the edge of the open plains, everybody was on the alert.

They emerged from the big trees and stopped among the young growth, looking out into the open country. About a mile away, a herd of game was grazing slowly westward. In the distance, they looked like the little horse-like things, no higher than a man's waist and heavily maned and bearded, that had been one of their most important sources of meat. For the ten thousandth time, Dard wished, as he strained his eyes, that somebody had thought to secure a pair of binoculars when they had abandoned the rocket-boat. He studied the grazing herd for a long time.

The seedling pines extended almost to the game-herd and would offer concealment for the approach, but the animals were grazing into the wind, and their scent was much keener than their vision. This would prelude one of their favorite hunting techniques, that of lurking in the high grass ahead of the quarry. It had rained heavily in the past few days, and the undermat of dead grass was soaked, making a fire-hunt impossible. Kalvar Dard knew that he could stalk to within easy carbine-shot, but he was unwilling to use cartridges on game; and in view of the proximity of Hairy People, he did not want to divide his band for a drive hunt.

"What's the scheme?" Analea asked him, realizing the problem as well as he did. "Do we try to take them from behind?"

"We'll take them from an angle," he decided. "We'll start from here and work in, closing on them at the rear of the herd. Unless the wind shifts on us, we ought to get within spear-cast. You and I will use the spears; Varnis can come along and cover for us with a carbine. Glav, you and Olva and Dorita stay here with the children and the packs. Keep a sharp lookout; Hairy People around, somewhere." He unslung his rifle and exchanged it for Olva's spears. "We can only eat about two of them before the meat begins to spoil, but kill all you can," he told Analea; "we need the skins."

Then he and the two girls began their slow, cautious, stalk. As long as the grassland was dotted with young trees, they walked upright, making good time, but the last five hundred yards they had to crawl, stopping often to check the wind, while the horse-herd drifted slowly by. Then they were directly behind the herd, with the wind in their faces, and they advanced more rapidly.

"Close enough?" Dard whispered to Analea.

"Yes; I'm taking the one that's lagging a little behind."

"I'm taking the one on the left of it." Kalvar Dard fitted a javelin to the hook of his throwing-stick. "Ready? Now!"

He leaped to his feet, drawing back his right arm and hurling, the throwing-stick giving added velocity to the spear. Beside him, he was conscious of Analea rising and propelling her spear. His missile caught the little bearded pony in the chest; it stumbled and fell forward to its front knees. He snatched another light spear, set it on the hook of the stick and darted it at another horse, which reared, biting at the spear with its teeth. Grabbing the heavy stabbing-spear, he ran forward, finishing it off with a heart-thrust. As he did, Varnis slung her carbine, snatched a stone-headed throwing axe from her belt, and knocked down another horse, then ran forward with her dagger to finish it.

By this time, the herd, alarmed, had stampeded and was galloping away, leaving the dead and dying behind. He and Analea had each killed two; with the one Varnis had knocked down, that made five. Using his dagger, he finished off one that was still kicking on the ground, and then began pulling out the throwing-spears. The girls, shouting in unison, were announcing the successful completion of the hunt; Glav, Olva, and Dorita were coming forward with the children.

*   *   *   *   *

It was sunset by the time they had finished the work of skinning and cutting up the horses and had carried the hide-wrapped bundles of meat to the little brook where they had intended camping. There was firewood to be gathered, and the meal to be cooked, and they were all tired.

"We can't do this very often, any more," Kalvar Dard told them, "but we might as well, tonight. Don't bother rubbing sticks for fire; I'll use the lighter."

He got it from a pouch on his belt--a small, gold-plated, atomic lighter, bearing the crest of his old regiment of the Frontier Guards. It was the last one they had, in working order. Piling a handful of dry splinters under the firewood, he held the lighter to it, pressed the activator, and watched the fire eat into the wood.

The greatest achievement of man's civilization, the mastery of the basic, cosmic, power of the atom--being used to kindle a fire of natural fuel, to cook unseasoned meat killed with stone-tipped spears. Dard looked sadly at the twinkling little gadget, then slipped it back into its pouch. Soon it would be worn out, like the other two, and then they would gain fire only by rubbing dry sticks, or hacking sparks from bits of flint or pyrites. Soon, too, the last cartridge would be fired, and then they would perforce depend for protection, as they were already doing for food, upon their spears.

And they were so helpless. Six adults, burdened with seven little children, all of them requiring momently care and watchfulness. If the cartridges could be made to last until they were old enough to fend for themselves.... If they could avoid collisions with the Hairy People.... Some day, they would be numerous enough for effective mutual protection and support; some day, the ratio of helpless children to able adults would redress itself. Until then, all that they could do would be to survive; day after day, they must follow the game-herds.

4

For twenty years, now, they had been following the game. Winters had come, with driving snow, forcing horses and deer into the woods, and the little band of humans to the protection of mountain caves. Springtime followed, with fresh grass on the plains and plenty of meat for the people of Kalvar Dard. Autumns followed summers, with fire-hunts, and the smoking and curing of meat and hides. Winters followed autumns, and springtimes came again, and thus until the twentieth year after the landing of the rocket-boat.

Kalvar Dard still walked in the lead, his hair and beard flecked with gray, but he no longer carried the heavy rifle; the last cartridge for that had been fired long ago. He carried the hand-axe, fitted with a long helve, and a spear with a steel head that had been worked painfully from the receiver of a useless carbine. He still had his pistol, with eight cartridges in the magazine, and his dagger, and the bomb-bag, containing the big demolition-bomb and one grenade. The last shred of clothing from the ship was gone, now; he was clad in a sleeveless tunic of skin and horsehide buskins.

Analea no longer walked beside him; eight years before, she had broken her back in a fall. It had been impossible to move her, and she stabbed herself with her dagger to save a cartridge. Seldar Glav had broken through the ice while crossing a river, and had lost his rifle; the next day he died of the chill he had taken. Olva had been killed by the Hairy People, the night they had attacked the camp, when Varnis' child had been killed.

They had beaten off that attack, shot or speared ten of the huge sub-men, and the next morning they buried their dead after their custom, under cairns of stone. Varnis had watched the burial of her child with blank, uncomprehending eyes, then she had turned to Kalvar Dard and said something that had horrified him more than any wild outburst of grief could have.

"Come on, Dard; what are we doing this for? You promised you'd take us to Tareesh, where we'd have good houses, and machines, and all sorts of lovely things to eat and wear. I don't like this place, Dard; I want to go to Tareesh."

From that day on, she had wandered in merciful darkness. She had not been idiotic, or raving mad; she had just escaped from a reality that she could no longer bear.

Varnis, lost in her dream-world, and Dorita, hard-faced and haggard, were the only ones left, beside Kalvar Dard, of the original eight. But the band had grown, meanwhile, to more than fifteen. In the rear, in Seldar Glav's old place, the son of Kalvar Dard and Analea walked. Like his father, he wore a pistol, for which he had six rounds, and a dagger, and in his hand he carried a stone-headed killing-maul with a three-foot handle which he had made for himself. The woman who walked beside him and carried his spears was the daughter of Glav and Olva; in a net-bag on her back she carried their infant child. The first Tareeshan born of Tareeshan parents; Kalvar Dard often looked at his little grandchild during nights in camp and days on the trail, seeing, in that tiny fur-swaddled morsel of humanity, the meaning and purpose of all that he did. Of the older girls, one or two were already pregnant, now; this tiny threatened beachhead of humanity was expanding, gaining strength. Long after man had died out on Doorsha and the dying planet itself had become an arid waste, the progeny of this little band would continue to grow and to dominate the younger planet, nearer the sun. Some day, an even mightier civilization than the one he had left would rise here....

             *   *   *   *   *

All day the trail had wound upward into the mountains. Great cliffs loomed above them, and little streams spumed and dashed in rocky gorges below. All day, the Hairy People had followed, fearful to approach too close, unwilling to allow their enemies to escape. It had started when they had rushed the camp, at daybreak; they had been beaten off, at cost of almost all the ammunition, and the death of one child. No sooner had the tribe of Kalvar Dard taken the trail, however, than they had been pressing after them. Dard had determined to cross the mountains, and had led his people up a game-trail, leading toward the notch of a pass high against the skyline.

The shaggy ape-things seemed to have divined his purpose. Once or twice, he had seen hairy brown shapes dodging among the rocks and stunted trees to the left. They were trying to reach the pass ahead of him. Well, if they did.... He made a quick mental survey of his resources. His pistol, and his son's, and Dorita's, with eight, and six, and seven rounds. One grenade, and the big demolition bomb, too powerful to be thrown by hand, but which could be set for delayed explosion and dropped over a cliff or left behind to explode among pursuers. Five steel daggers, and plenty of spears and slings and axes. Himself, his son and his son's woman, Dorita, and four or five of the older boys and girls, who would make effective front-line fighters. And Varnis, who might come out of her private dream-world long enough to give account for herself, and even the tiniest of the walking children could throw stones or light spears. Yes, they could force the pass, if the Hairy People reached it ahead of them, and then seal it shut with the heavy bomb. What lay on the other side, he did not know; he wondered how much game there would be, and if there were Hairy People on that side, too.

Two shots slammed quickly behind him. He dropped his axe and took a two-hand grip on his stabbing-spear as he turned. His son was hurrying forward, his pistol drawn, glancing behind as he came.

"Hairy People. Four," he reported. "I shot two; she threw a spear and killed another. The other ran."

The daughter of Seldar Glav and Olva nodded in agreement.

"I had no time to throw again," she said, "and Bo-Bo would not shoot the one that ran."

Kalvar Dard's son, who had no other name than the one his mother had called him as a child, defended himself. "He was running away. It is the rule: *use bullets only to save life, where a spear will not serve*."

Kalvar Dard nodded. "You did right, son," he said, taking out his own pistol and removing the magazine, from which he extracted two cartridges. "Load these into your pistol; four rounds aren't enough. Now we each have six. Go back to the rear, keep the little ones moving, and don't let Varnis get behind."

"That is right. *We must all look out for Varnis, and take care of her*," the boy recited obediently. "That is the rule."

He dropped to the rear. Kalvar Dard holstered his pistol and picked up his axe, and the column moved forward again. They were following a ledge, now; on the left, there was a sheer drop of several hundred feet, and on the right a cliff rose above them, growing higher and steeper as the trail slanted upward. Dard was worried about the ledge; if it came to an end, they would all be trapped. No one would escape. He suddenly felt old and unutterably weary. It was a frightful weight that he bore--responsibility for an entire race.

*   *   *   *   *

Suddenly, behind him, Dorita fired her pistol upward. Dard sprang forward--there was no room for him to jump aside--and drew his pistol. The boy, Bo-Bo, was trying to find a target from his position in the rear. Then Dard saw the two Hairy People; the boy fired, and the stone fell, all at once.

It was a heavy stone, half as big as a man's torso, and it almost missed Kalvar Dard. If it had hit him directly, it would have killed him instantly, mashing him to a bloody pulp; as it was, he was knocked flat, the stone pinning his legs.

At Bo-Bo's shot, a hairy body plummeted down, to hit the ledge. Bo-Bo's woman instantly ran it through with one of her spears. The other ape-thing, the one Dorita had shot, was still clinging to a rock above. Two of the children scampered up to it and speared it repeatedly, screaming like little furies. Dorita and one of the older girls got the rock off Kalvar Dard's legs and tried to help him to his feet, but he collapsed, unable to stand. Both his legs were broken.

This was it, he thought, sinking back. "Dorita, I want you to run ahead and see what the trail's like," he said. "See if the ledge is passable. And find a place, not too far ahead, where we can block the trail by exploding that demolition-bomb. It has to be close enough for a couple of you to carry or drag me and get me there in one piece."

"What are you going to do?"

"What do you think?" he retorted. "I have both legs broken. You can't carry me with you; if you try it, they'll catch us and kill us all. I'll have to stay behind; I'll block the trail behind you, and get as many of them as I can, while I'm at it. Now, run along and do as I said."

She nodded. "I'll be back as soon as I can," she agreed.

The others were crowding around Dard. Bo-Bo bent over him, perplexed and worried. "What are you going to do, father?" he asked. "You are hurt. Are you going to go away and leave us, as mother did when she was hurt?"

"Yes, son; I'll have to. You carry me on ahead a little, when Dorita gets back, and leave me where she shows you to. I'm going to stay behind and block the trail, and kill a few Hairy People. I'll use the big bomb."

"The *big* bomb? The one nobody dares throw?" The boy looked at his father in wonder.

"That's right. Now, when you leave me, take the others and get away as fast as you can. Don't stop till you're up to the pass. Take my pistol and dagger, and the axe and the big spear, and take the little bomb, too. Take everything I have, only leave the big bomb with me. I'll need that."

Dorita rejoined them. "There's a waterfall ahead. We can get around it, and up to the pass. The way's clear and easy; if you put off the bomb just this side of it, you'll start a rock-slide that'll block everything."

"All right. Pick me up, a couple of you. Don't take hold of me below the knees. And hurry."

*   *   *   *   *

A hairy shape appeared on the ledge below them; one of the older boys used his throwing-stick to drive a javelin into it. Two of the girls picked up Dard; Bo-Bo and his woman gathered up the big spear and the axe and the bomb-bag.

They hurried forward, picking their way along the top of a talus of rubble at the foot of the cliff, and came to where the stream gushed out of a narrow gorge. The air was wet with spray there, and loud with the roar of the waterfall. Kalvar Dard looked around; Dorita had chosen the spot well. Not even a sure-footed mountain-goat could make the ascent, once that gorge was blocked.

"All right; put me down here," he directed. "Bo-Bo, take my belt, and give me the big bomb. You have one light grenade; know how to use it?"

"Of course, you have often showed me. I turn the top, and then press in the little thing on the side, and hold it in till I throw. I throw it at least a spear-cast, and drop to the ground or behind something."

"That's right. And use it only in greatest danger, to save everybody. Spare your cartridges; use them only to save life. And save everything of metal, no matter how small."

"Yes. Those are the rules. I will follow them, and so will the others. And we will always take care of Varnis."

"Well, goodbye, son." He gripped the boy's hand. "Now get everybody out of here; don't stop till you're at the pass."

"You're not staying behind!" Varnis cried. "Dard, you promised us! I remember, when we were all in the ship together--you and I and Analea and Olva and Dorita and Eldra and, oh, what was that other girl's name, Kyna! And we were all having such a nice time, and you were telling us how we'd all come to Tareesh, and we were having such fun talking about it...."

"That's right, Varnis," he agreed. "And so I will. I have something to do, here, but I'll meet you on top of the mountain, after I'm through, and in the morning we'll all go to Tareesh."

She smiled--the gentle, childlike smile of the harmlessly mad--and turned away. The son of Kalvar Dard made sure that she and all the children were on the way, and then he, too, turned and followed them, leaving Dard alone.

Alone, with a bomb and a task. He'd borne that task for twenty years, now; in a few minutes, it would be ended, with an instant's searing heat. He tried not to be too glad; there were so many things he might have done, if he had tried harder. Metals, for instance. Somewhere there surely must be ores which they could have smelted, but he had never found them. And he might have tried catching some of the little horses they hunted for food, to break and train to bear burdens. And the alphabet--why hadn't he taught it to Bo-Bo and the daughter of Seldar Glav, and laid on them an obligation to teach the others? And the grass-seeds they used for making flour sometimes; they should have planted fields of the better kinds, and patches of edible roots, and returned at the proper time to harvest them. There were so many things, things that none of those young savages or their children would think of in ten thousand years....

Something was moving among the rocks, a hundred yards away. He straightened, as much as his broken legs would permit, and watched. Yes, there was one of them, and there was another, and another. One rose from behind a rock and came forward at a shambling run, making bestial sounds. Then two more lumbered into sight, and in a moment the ravine was alive with them. They were almost upon him when Kalvar Dard pressed in the thumbpiece of the bomb; they were clutching at him when he released it. He felt a slight jar....

*　　*　　*　　*　　*

When they reached the pass, they all stopped as the son of Kalvar Dard turned and looked back. Dorita stood beside him, looking toward the waterfall too; she also knew what was about to happen. The others merely gaped in blank incomprehension, or grasped their weapons, thinking that the enemy was pressing close behind and that they were making a stand here. A few of the smaller boys and girls began picking up stones.

Then a tiny pin-point of brilliance winked, just below where the snow-fed stream vanished into the gorge. That was all, for an instant, and then a great fire-shot cloud swirled upward, hundreds of feet into the air; there was a crash, louder than any sound any of them except Dorita and Varnis had ever heard before.

"He did it!" Dorita said softly.

"Yes, he did it. My father was a brave man," Bo-Bo replied. "We are safe, now."

Varnis, shocked by the explosion, turned and stared at him, and then she laughed happily. "Why, there you are, Dard!" she exclaimed. "I was wondering where you'd gone. What did you do, after we left?"

"What do you mean?" The boy was puzzled, not knowing how much he looked like his father, when his father had been an officer of the Frontier Guards, twenty years before.

His puzzlement worried Varnis vaguely. "You.... You are Dard, aren't you?" she asked. "But that's silly; of course you're Dard! Who else could you be?"

"Yes. I am Dard," the boy said, remembering that it was the rule for everybody to be kind to Varnis and to pretend to agree with her. Then another thought struck him. His shoulders straightened. "Yes. I am Dard, son of Dard," he told them all. "I lead, now. Does anybody say no?"

He shifted his axe and spear to his left hand and laid his right hand on the butt of his pistol, looking sternly at Dorita. If any of them tried to dispute his claim, it would be she. But instead, she gave him the nearest thing to a real smile that had crossed her face in years.

"You are Dard," she told him; "you lead us, now."

"But of course Dard leads! Hasn't he always led us?" Varnis wanted to know. "Then what's all the argument about? And tomorrow he's going to take us to Tareesh, and we'll have houses and ground-cars and aircraft and gardens and lights, and all the lovely things we want. Aren't you, Dard?"

"Yes, Varnis; I will take you all to Tareesh, to all the wonderful things," Dard, son of Dard, promised, for such was the rule about Varnis.

Then he looked down from the pass into the country beyond. There were lower mountains, below, and foothills, and a wide blue valley, and, beyond that, distant peaks reared jaggedly against the sky. He pointed with his father's axe.

"We go down that way," he said.

*   *   *   *   *

So they went, down, and on, and on, and on. The last cartridge was fired; the last sliver of Doorshan metal wore out or rusted away. By then, however, they had learned to make chipped stone, and bone, and reindeer-horn, serve their needs. Century after century, millennium after millennium, they followed the game-herds from birth to death, and birth replenished their numbers faster than death depleted. Bands grew in numbers and split; young men rebelled against the rule of the old and took their women and children elsewhere.

They hunted down the hairy Neanderthalers, and exterminated them ruthlessly, the origin of their implacable hatred lost in legend. All that they remembered, in the misty, confused, way that one remembers a dream, was that there had once been a time of happiness and plenty, and that there was a goal to which they would some day attain. They left the mountains--were they the Caucasus? The Alps? The Pamirs?--and spread outward, conquering as they went.

We find their bones, and their stone weapons, and their crude paintings, in the caves of Cro-Magnon and Grimaldi and Altimira and Mas-d'Azil; the deep layers of horse and reindeer and mammoth bones at their feasting-place at Solutre. We wonder how and whence a race so like our own came into a world of brutish sub-humans.

Just as we wonder, too, at the network of canals which radiate from the polar caps of our sister planet, and speculate on the possibility that they were the work of hands like our own. And we concoct elaborate jokes about the "Men From Mars"-- ***ourselves***.

The End

*   *   *   *   *

The Codes Of Hammurabi And Moses
W. W. Davies

QTY

The discovery of the Hammurabi Code is one of the greatest achievements of archaeology, and is of paramount interest, not only to the student of the Bible, but also to all those interested in ancient history...

Religion   **ISBN:** *1-59462-338-4*   **Pages:132**

MSRP $12.95

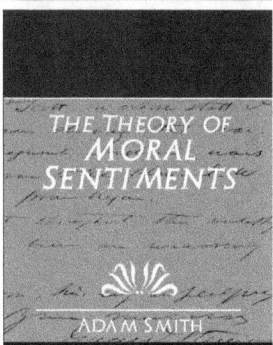

The Theory of Moral Sentiments
Adam Smith

QTY

This work from 1749. contains original theories of conscience amd moral judgment and it is the foundation for systemof morals.

Philosophy **ISBN:** *1-59462-777-0*   **Pages:536**

MSRP $19.95

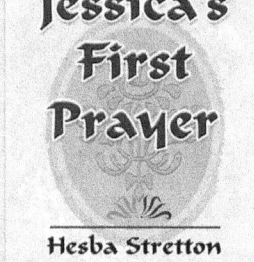

Jessica's First Prayer
Hesba Stretton

QTY

In a screened and secluded corner of one of the many railway-bridges which span the streets of London there could be seen a few years ago, from five o'clock every morning until half past eight, a tidily set-out coffee-stall, consisting of a trestle and board, upon which stood two large tin cans, with a small fire of charcoal burning under each so as to keep the coffee boiling during the early hours of the morning when the work-people were thronging into the city on their way to their daily toil...

Pages:84

Childrens   **ISBN:** *1-59462-373-2*   *MSRP $9.95*

My Life and Work
Henry Ford

QTY

Henry Ford revolutionized the world with his implementation of mass production for the Model T automobile. Gain valuable business insight into his life and work with his own auto-biography... "We have only started on our development of our country we have not as yet, with all our talk of wonderful progress, done more than scratch the surface. The progress has been wonderful enough but..."

Pages:300

Biographies/   **ISBN:** *1-59462-198-5*   *MSRP $21.95*

The Art of Cross-Examination
Francis Wellman

QTY

I presume it is the experience of every author, after his first book is published upon an important subject, to be almost overwhelmed with a wealth of ideas and illustrations which could readily have been included in his book, and which to his own mind, at least, seem to make a second edition inevitable. Such certainly was the case with me; and when the first edition had reached its sixth impression in five months, I rejoiced to learn that it seemed to my publishers that the book had met with a sufficiently favorable reception to justify a second and considerably enlarged edition. ..

Pages:412

Reference   **ISBN: *1-59462-647-2***   *MSRP $19.95*

On the Duty of Civil Disobedience
Henry David Thoreau

QTY

Thoreau wrote his famous essay, On the Duty of Civil Disobedience, as a protest against an unjust but popular war and the immoral but popular institution of slave-owning. He did more than write—he declined to pay his taxes, and was hauled off to gaol in consequence. Who can say how much this refusal of his hastened the end of the war and of slavery ?

Law   **ISBN: *1-59462-747-9***   **Pages:48**

MSRP $7.45

Dream Psychology Psychoanalysis for Beginners
Sigmund Freud

QTY

Sigmund Freud, born Sigismund Schlomo Freud (May 6, 1856 - September 23, 1939), was a Jewish-Austrian neurologist and psychiatrist who co-founded the psychoanalytic school of psychology. Freud is best known for his theories of the unconscious mind, especially involving the mechanism of repression; his redefinition of sexual desire as mobile and directed towards a wide variety of objects; and his therapeutic techniques, especially his understanding of transference in the therapeutic relationship and the presumed value of dreams as sources of insight into unconscious desires.

Pages:196

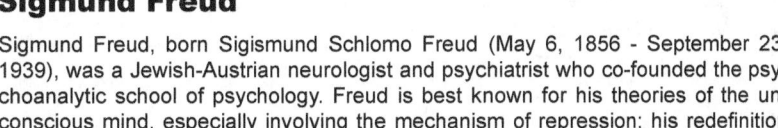

Psychology   **ISBN: *1-59462-905-6***   *MSRP $15.45*

The Miracle of Right Thought
Orison Swett Marden

QTY

Believe with all of your heart that you will do what you were made to do. When the mind has once formed the habit of holding cheerful, happy, prosperous pictures, it will not be easy to form the opposite habit. It does not matter how improbable or how far away this realization may see, or how dark the prospects may be, if we visualize them as best we can, as vividly as possible, hold tenaciously to them and vigorously struggle to attain them, they will gradually become actualized, realized in the life. But a desire, a longing without endeavor, a yearning abandoned or held indifferently will vanish without realization.

Pages:360

Self Help   **ISBN: *1-59462-644-8***   *MSRP $25.45*

www.bookjungle.com *email: sales@bookjungle.com fax: 630-214-0564 mail: Book Jungle PO Box 2226 Champaign, IL 61825*

QTY

The Rosicrucian Cosmo-Conception Mystic Christianity *by Max Heindel*　　ISBN: *1-59462-188-8*　**$38.95**
The Rosicrucian Cosmo-conception is not dogmatic, neither does it appeal to any other authority than the reason of the student. It is: not controversial, but is: sent forth in the, hope that it may help to clear...　　New Age/Religion Pages 646

Abandonment To Divine Providence *by Jean-Pierre de Caussade*　　ISBN: *1-59462-228-0*　**$25.95**
"The Rev. Jean Pierre de Caussade was one of the most remarkable spiritual writers of the Society of Jesus in France in the 18th Century. His death took place at Toulouse in 1751. His works have gone through many editions and have been republished...　　Inspirational/Religion Pages 400

Mental Chemistry *by Charles Haanel*　　ISBN: *1-59462-192-6*　**$23.95**
Mental Chemistry allows the change of material conditions by combining and appropriately utilizing the power of the mind. Much like applied chemistry creates something new and unique out of careful combinations of chemicals the mastery of mental chemistry...　　New Age Pages 354

The Letters of Robert Browning and Elizabeth Barret Barrett 1845-1846 vol II　　ISBN: *1-59462-193-4*　**$35.95**
by Robert Browning and Elizabeth Barrett　　Biographies Pages 596

Gleanings In Genesis (volume I) *by Arthur W. Pink*　　ISBN: *1-59462-130-6*　**$27.45**
Appropriately has Genesis been termed "the seed plot of the Bible" for in it we have, in germ form, almost all of the great doctrines which are afterwards fully developed in the books of Scripture which follow...　　Religion/Inspirational Pages 420

The Master Key *by L. W. de Laurence*　　ISBN: *1-59462-001-6*　**$30.95**
In no branch of human knowledge has there been a more lively increase of the spirit of research during the past few years than in the study of Psychology, Concentration and Mental Discipline. The requests for authentic lessons in Thought Control, Mental Discipline and...　　New Age/Business Pages 422

The Lesser Key Of Solomon Goetia *by L. W. de Laurence*　　ISBN: *1-59462-092-X*　**$9.95**
This translation of the first book of the "Lernegton" which is now for the first time made accessible to students of Talismanic Magic was done, after careful collation and edition, from numerous Ancient Manuscripts in Hebrew, Latin, and French...　　New Age/Occult Pages 92

Rubaiyat Of Omar Khayyam *by Edward Fitzgerald*　　ISBN:*1-59462-332-5*　**$13.95**
Edward Fitzgerald, whom the world has already learned, in spite of his own efforts to remain within the shadow of anonymity, to look upon as one of the rarest poets of the century, was born at Bredfield, in Suffolk, on the 31st of March, 1809. He was the third son of John Purcell...　　Music Pages 172

Ancient Law *by Henry Maine*　　ISBN: *1-59462-128-4*　**$29.95**
The chief object of the following pages is to indicate some of the earliest ideas of mankind, as they are reflected in Ancient Law, and to point out the relation of those ideas to modern thought.　　Religion/History Pages 452

Far-Away Stories *by William J. Locke*　　ISBN: *1-59462-129-2*　**$19.45**
"Good wine needs no bush, but a collection of mixed vintages does. And this book is just such a collection. Some of the stories I do not want to remain buried for ever in the museum files of dead magazine-numbers an author's not unpardonable vanity..."　　Fiction Pages 272

Life of David Crockett *by David Crockett*　　ISBN: *1-59462-250-7*　**$27.45**
"Colonel David Crockett was one of the most remarkable men of the times in which he lived. Born in humble life, but gifted with a strong will, an indomitable courage, and unremitting perseverance...　　Biographies/New Age Pages 424

Lip-Reading *by Edward Nitchie*　　ISBN: *1-59462-206-X*　**$25.95**
Edward B. Nitchie, founder of the New York School for the Hard of Hearing, now the Nitchie School of Lip-Reading, Inc, wrote "LIP-READING Principles and Practice". The development and perfecting of this meritorious work on lip-reading was an undertaking...　　How-to Pages 400

A Handbook of Suggestive Therapeutics, Applied Hypnotism, Psychic Science　　ISBN: *1-59462-214-0*　**$24.95**
by Henry Munro　　Health/New Age/Health/Self-help Pages 376

A Doll's House: and Two Other Plays *by Henrik Ibsen*　　ISBN: *1-59462-112-8*　**$19.95**
Henrik Ibsen created this classic when in revolutionary 1848 Rome. Introducing some striking concepts in playwriting for the realist genre, this play has been studied the world over.　　Fiction/Classics/Plays 308

The Light of Asia *by sir Edwin Arnold*　　ISBN: *1-59462-204-3*　**$13.95**
In this poetic masterpiece, Edwin Arnold describes the life and teachings of Buddha. The man who was to become known as Buddha to the world was born as Prince Gautama of India but he rejected the worldly riches and abandoned the reigns of power when...　　Religion/History/Biographies Pages 170

The Complete Works of Guy de Maupassant *by Guy de Maupassant*　　ISBN: *1-59462-157-8*　**$16.95**
"For days and days, nights and nights, I had dreamed of that first kiss which was to consecrate our engagement, and I knew not on what spot I should put my lips..."　　Fiction/Classics Pages 240

The Art of Cross-Examination *by Francis L. Wellman*　　ISBN: *1-59462-309-0*　**$26.95**
Written by a renowned trial lawyer, Wellman imparts his experience and uses case studies to explain how to use psychology to extract desired information through questioning.　　How-to/Science/Reference Pages 408

Answered or Unanswered? *by Louisa Vaughan*　　ISBN: *1-59462-248-5*　**$10.95**
Miracles of Faith in China　　Religion Pages 112

The Edinburgh Lectures on Mental Science (1909) *by Thomas*　　ISBN: *1-59462-008-3*　**$11.95**
This book contains the substance of a course of lectures recently given by the writer in the Queen Street Hall, Edinburgh. Its purpose is to indicate the Natural Principles governing the relation between Mental Action and Material Conditions...　　New Age/Psychology Pages 148

Ayesha *by H. Rider Haggard*　　ISBN: *1-59462-301-5*　**$24.95**
Verily and indeed it is the unexpected that happens! Probably if there was one person upon the earth from whom the Editor of this, and of a certain previous history, did not expect to hear again...　　Classics Pages 380

Ayala's Angel *by Anthony Trollope*　　ISBN: *1-59462-352-X*　**$29.95**
The two girls were both pretty, but Lucy who was twenty-one who supposed to be simple and comparatively unattractive, whereas Ayala was credited, as her Bombwhat romantic name might show, with poetic charm and a taste for romance. Ayala when her father died was nineteen...　　Fiction Pages 484

The American Commonwealth *by James Bryce*　　ISBN: *1-59462-286-8*　**$34.45**
An interpretation of American democratic political theory. It examines political mechanics and society from the perspective of Scotsman James Bryce　　Politics Pages 572

Stories of the Pilgrims *by Margaret P. Pumphrey*　　ISBN: *1-59462-116-0*　**$17.95**
This book explores pilgrims religious oppression in England as well as their escape to Holland and eventual crossing to America on the Mayflower, and their early days in New England...　　History Pages 268

QTY

The Fasting Cure *by Sinclair Upton*   ISBN: *1-59462-222-1* **$13.95**
In the Cosmopolitan Magazine for May, 1910, and in the Contemporary Review (London) for April, 1910, I published an article dealing with my experiences in fasting. I have written a great many magazine articles, but never one which attracted so much attention... New Age/Self Help/Health Pages 164

Hebrew Astrology *by Sepharial*   ISBN: *1-59462-308-2* **$13.45**
In these days of advanced thinking it is a matter of common observation that we have left many of the old landmarks behind and that we are now pressing forward to greater heights and to a wider horizon than that which represented the mind-content of our progenitors... Astrology Pages 144

Thought Vibration or The Law of Attraction in the Thought World   ISBN: *1-59462-127-6* **$12.95**
by William Walker Atkinson   Psychology/Religion Pages 144

Optimism *by Helen Keller*   ISBN: *1-59462-108-X* **$15.95**
Helen Keller was blind, deaf, and mute since 19 months old, yet famously learned how to overcome these handicaps, communicate with the world, and spread her lectures promoting optimism. An inspiring read for everyone... Biographies/Inspirational Pages 84

Sara Crewe *by Frances Burnett*   ISBN: *1-59462-360-0* **$9.45**
In the first place, Miss Minchin lived in London. Her home was a large, dull, tall one, in a large, dull square, where all the houses were alike, and all the sparrows were alike, and where all the door-knockers made the same heavy sound... Childrens/Classic Pages 88

The Autobiography of Benjamin Franklin *by Benjamin Franklin*   ISBN: *1-59462-135-7* **$24.95**
The Autobiography of Benjamin Franklin has probably been more extensively read than any other American historical work, and no other book of its kind has had such ups and downs of fortune. Franklin lived for many years in England, where he was agent... Biographies/History Pages 332

Name	
Email	
Telephone	
Address	
City, State ZIP	

☐ **Credit Card**   ☐ **Check / Money Order**

Credit Card Number	
Expiration Date	
Signature	

Please Mail to: Book Jungle
PO Box 2226
Champaign, IL 61825
or Fax to: 630-214-0564

ORDERING INFORMATION

web: *www.bookjungle.com*
email: *sales@bookjungle.com*
fax: *630-214-0564*
mail: *Book Jungle PO Box 2226 Champaign, IL 61825*
or PayPal *to sales@bookjungle.com*

Please contact us for bulk discounts

DIRECT-ORDER TERMS

**20% Discount if You Order
Two or More Books**
Free Domestic Shipping!
Accepted: Master Card, Visa,
Discover, American Express